Brenna Lyons

THE *Consort*

THE FANTASY CLUB #1

Blurb

Liz is a lonely woman, widowed before she was properly a bride. Ben was the only man for her. Now he's gone, and she has been left in agony, both physical and emotional.

Patrice has long-ago decided she's asexual. Though she tried to play the games to fit in, she's never found anyone sexually appealing.

When these two friends each receive an invitation to the exclusive *Fantasy Club*, they decide to go, just to satisfy their interfering friends…whichever of them spent the money to send them to the club. Once there, they learn about the true magic of the club. It's not called Little Olympus for kicks. But, can even the gods of Olympus make a happily ever after for two lost causes like these?

This book is written in US English.

PUBLISHER

Dedication

To Tamer, the one I was born for.

Chapter One

The Fantasy Club, Opening Night

Jack Jupiter looked out over the assembled members and clients in his office. "The rules are understood?" he asked solemnly.

"You're certain your wards will be strong enough?" Steven asked. "If they're not—"

Jupe raised a hand to still his words of caution. "You are not the first of your kind to seek this," he assured the Beast. "The Warriors cannot enter the grounds."

He smiled weakly. "What would I have to do to stay here permanently?"

"Because your gods will not permit it, I cannot grant you that."

"I know." He sighed in defeat, much as every Beast Jupe had met had done. "The Stone permits us only the night."

"I am afraid so."

Jupe scanned his gaze to the next man in line. He nodded silently. They had discussed his fantasy many times over the years he'd worked in the club, and the time was right.

Still, this would be the greatest challenge the Fantasy Club had encountered in a century or more. Jupe prayed the interplay of attendees would work out as planned. If it didn't, they might fail, for the first time in the history of the club.

He focused his attention on Michael.

The young man shifted nervously. "Will this really work?"

Jupe chuckled. The human members were always hardest to convince. The otherworldly members never doubted what Jupe and his staff were capable of. "Assuredly. Are you certain this is your wish?"

"Absolutely."

"Then it is as good as done."

He smiled and managed a shaky nod.

The one female member in presence, Elise, didn't question Jupe. Her membership was an inheritance, passed down, mother to daughter for generations, a gift from an esteemed relative.

"Elise?" he prodded her. The members or clients had to agree to the rules for the contract to be binding.

She nodded. "He is the right one."

"If the forms have been observed, you cannot be mistaken."

"They have," she assured him.

"Then this meeting is ended. Steven, my staff has found your match, as promised. The rest of you may leave the details in the outer office, if you have not already done so.

They left quietly. No discussion was exchanged between the members. Fantasies were a private matter.

Just as it should be.

Jupe glanced at the final member in the room, the one the others hadn't noticed. "She has been sent for, my friend. You have my word."

Rain didn't answer. He didn't need to answer. A slight tip of his head was all Jupe needed to see.

* * * *

Jupe stopped cold at the sight of his old friend. Eric stared out at the expansive gardens. Rather, he stared through the gardens to some faraway place where a woman waited for a package Jupe had sent to her only moments ago.

Eric lived in the Fantasy Club, as Jupe and a few dozen other staff members did, at least part time. Over the years, his old friend had taken advantage of the club's services to fill his needs many times.

"But it never sticks," Eric grumbled, proving he could hear Jupe's inner monologue.

Jupe sighed. "No. It never does. Maybe this time..." But he didn't continue.

"It's ironic, you know. I match so many couples, but I'm pretty much a failure when it comes to my own relationships."

"I wouldn't call you a failure," Jupe protested. "How long did your last—"

Eric turned on him. "Not long enough." His eyes were shadowed, and his skin pale.

This is what not having a woman does to him. Jupe's heart ached. He hated seeing Eric suffer this way.

"Why am I trying this again?" he complained. "Just once, I should roll over and pretend I don't care."

Jupe choked on that thought. "You know you have to." He calmed himself. He had no right to ask Eric to go through this again. "I...I mean, eventually. You have time. I can call the invitation back. It doesn't have to be this year."

Eric shook his head. "You know I am nothing without a consort. I've delayed too long. It's time."

Jupe tipped his head in a bow. "As you wish. I'll make sure the invitations go, then."

Eric shoved his fists in his pants pockets and turned to stare out at the gardens again, waiting.

Waiting for the magic to return to his life.

For as long as it lasts.

Chapter Two
The Consort

Liz stared at the card in shock. "You are hereby issued an invitation to *The Fantasy Club's Valentine's Day Costume Ball*. The event will take place at nine o'clock on February the thirteenth. A car will arrive promptly at eight to collect you and your escort. Please dress in the costume that will be provided for you."

She dropped into a kitchen chair woodenly. "Which one of them did this to me?" she moaned. *More importantly, how do I call it off?*

Liz didn't care if the person who did this got a refund for her investment or not. *She shouldn't have done it in the first place!* She fumed at the situation.

I don't want a fantasy man. Liz wanted Ben, but Ben was beyond her reach now.

She skated a fingertip along the scar under her hair. She had several others that were more visible and disfiguring. *What man would find that appealing?*

No. I won't defile Ben's memory. He was the only man for me. There will never be another.

An energetic knock dragged Liz back to the present. She headed to the door like a woman condemned.

What else would I call this "gift"?

Pat's usually glittering green eyes were hard, a sure sign that she was hacked at someone. She flounced in, her red curls bouncing. Four steps into the condo, Pat turned on her heel, waved a cream colored envelope that looked all too familiar under Liz's nose, and raised an eyebrow in challenge.

"Oh no," Liz breathed.

"Okay. Spill it. What fantasy did you tell them to give me? Or you, for that matter? Don't get me wrong. I have nothing against you having a fantasy, but me? Liz, really."

She groaned. "Tell me you did do this to me," she pleaded. "Tell me it can be called off." It wasn't something Liz would expect from Pat. In fact, Pat was the only one of their friends who respected and openly supported Liz's decision.

But, if it's not Pat, I have no hope of finding out who it is in time to end this farce before there's a public scene about it.

* * * *

Pat winced at the sight of the tears pooling in Liz's eyes. "You really didn't set this up, in some romantic push to help me find Mr. Right?"

"I'm afraid not. You know our deal." She sighed and ran a hand through her mussed hair.

Pat nodded. She knew their deal well enough. She stayed out of Liz's love life and Liz stayed out of hers.

Nonexistent though they both are. But we know that's for the best.

"Which one of them do you think did this?" Liz asked, a hair off desperate by Pat's estimation.

"I couldn't tell you for sure. You're the only one with enough money to pull this off I know. The Fantasy Club doesn't come cheap. Or so I've heard."

"And what *have* you heard?"

"That my spending money for the next three years wouldn't pay for one of us, let alone two."

Liz rubbed at her forehead roughly, most likely coming down with another of her migraines. Stress did that to her. "What did your invitation say?"

"That I was to escort you to the ball, so I naturally thought you arranged it." Pat realized how ridiculous that sounded, even as it emerged from her mouth.

"Oh, please, Pat. Me? Be serious for a minute." Liz went to the fridge and pulled out a Coke. She retrieved ibuprofen from the cabinet, popped open the can and the bottle of medicine, then took the painkillers down with a mouthful of soda.

"I should have known." Liz was the last person Pat should have suspected of this. She sank into one of the chairs at the kitchen table. "What fantasies do you think they asked for?"

Liz lowered herself into the chair next to Pat with a grimace. Was it her injuries, her headache, or the thought of having someone do this to her? There was no way to be sure.

"Can't they just leave us alone?" Liz moaned. Her freckled nose scrunched in distaste.

"Obviously not. It's probably Karen or Jane, you know." That particular duo had always been outspoken in their beliefs that the right men would cure all Liz's and Pat's ills—make Liz forget Ben and convince Pat that sex was more than a ho-hum experience.

"I know."

The defeat in her friend's tone snapped Pat's resolve. Someone was going to pay for this. "No man is going to make my toes curl," she asserted hotly. "And no man can replace Ben."

"I know it. I just wish Karen and Jane knew it."

It has to be one of them. But how could either of them afford this?

"Should we refuse to go?" Liz asked, seemingly perking up at the idea. "I mean…they can't force us to. Can they?"

"Not without committing a kidnapping or two…and possibly assault." Pat ran her finger along the edge of the invitation. "No. We'll meet these guys and turn them down gracefully and completely. Then Karen and Jane will know we tried. Or…" She sighed. "At least that we didn't chicken out and waste the invitations."

It was a solid bet nothing could come of the invitations, after all. Clearly, Karen and Jane knew *nothing* about either of them.

Liz went a few shades paler. "On one condition."

"Anything. Just name it." She knew expecting Liz to attend was asking a lot of her best friend, but they had to get the Matchmaking Duo off their cases somehow.

"Don't you dare leave my side." She trembled a bit at that.

"Okay. Sounds like a plan." Smart dating these days pretty much demanded that anyway. You never knew what a man might do, left alone with a woman who didn't know him.

"What do you suppose our costumes will be?"

Pat shrugged. "I guess we'll find out when they arrive."

Chapter Three

Pat winced at the sight of Liz. Her friend's cheeks were raw and tear-stained.

And she still isn't dressed. No way am I going alone. No way. She checked her watch, groaning. "We decided we'd both do this," Pat commented calmly.

Calm was essential. Liz had enough problems with anxiety since she lost Ben. Adding more stress was something Pat would never do to her.

"I-I can't. This is some sort of sick joke!" Liz stopped short of stomping her foot in frustration, Pat was sure.

She closed the door, abruptly concerned. Whatever had upset Liz this time, it was beyond the norm. "What's wrong? What happened?"

Liz pointed a shaking finger at the huge box on the countertop. "That," she spat in supreme distaste. "I will not wear that *thing*."

Pat furrowed her brow in confusion. She strode to the box and dragged the lid off, then dropped it to the floor with a curse. "Oh no. They didn't dare." But clearly someone *had* dared.

"They did," Liz confirmed with a hitch that could only be a sob. "I won't wear it, Pat. I won't. Fuck them."

Pat retrieved the lid and covered the box, furious. *Whoever did this is a dead man. Uh...woman. Whatever.* It was a solemn vow. "A wedding dress," she growled aloud. "You are absolutely right. You're not wearing that."

"And I'm not going," Liz insisted.

"Oh yes, we most certainly are going. Someone has to pay for this. Someone is *going* to regret it."

"B-but—"

"But what?" Whatever Liz's reason, Pat intended to talk her out of it. There was about to be one hell of a reckoning, and Liz was going to get to see it first-hand.

"The invitation said—"

"Fuck the invitation. For that matter, the invitation *requested* you dress in what they sent. That means you are free to deny their request." *Let's get legalistic.* She had to do something to snap Liz out of her near-panic state.

Liz stared at her in open-mouthed shock for several heartbeats, then burst out laughing.

That's better. Pat tried to control the smile pulling up at her lips, but she finally gave up and laughed long and hard. If Liz wasn't wallowing in self-pity, she had a chance to avenge them both. Someone at the Fantasy Club was about to pay for upsetting Liz this way. *Followed by one of their* former *friends. It will be my pleasure to dish that out.*

"Yeah," Liz managed through red-faced giggles. "Fuck them. What are they going to do to me? Send me home?" That warranted another spate of laughter.

"Maybe so, but that's where we want to be anyway. If we get out of there early enough, maybe we'll stop for dinner somewhere, so as not to waste the outfits. Once I rip them a new one, of course."

"More information than I need about your intentions." Liz smiled. "You know, watching you in a full fury will be kind of fun. Haven't seen that in a while."

Pat threaded her arm through Liz's and led her toward the bedroom. "A show you won't want to miss. Now, let's go pick out your real outfit."

Liz nodded her agreement, though her smile went brittle at the reminder. She fretted over her choices for most of the half hour they had to spare. Pat grimaced at that. Being in a social cocoon of sorts, Liz hadn't had any reason to keep a closet full of clothes designed for formal or semi-formal occasions.

And she donated many of her short dresses, because they showed the scars around her knee.

Finally, Liz pulled a garment bag from the back of the closet. She bit her lower lip, surveying the three dresses inside.

Dresses that marked special occasions with Ben. Pat had seen them before. The brick red was from their first date. *She won't choose that one. It's short and will show the scars.* The hunter green was from the first time they had sex. *That one is a possibility, but it's not all that dressy. Liz will want to put her best foot forward. If for no other reason, being dressed to the nines will give her confidence.*

As if Liz had come to all the same conclusions Pat had, she pulled out the blue velvet.

From the night Ben asked her to marry him.

Liz took a calming breath.

Her heart aching, Pat covered Liz's hand with her own. "You don't have to, honey."

"I do. It's my only formal gown."

"Don't go formal, if you don't want to. Fuck them, remember?"

Liz straightened her spine. "What better to wear while I turn down some guy trying to take Ben's place?"

Good. She's in the right frame of mind. "If that's what you want, sweetie, I say we go all out."

She looked to the diamond solitaire she still wore. "It is."

Liz didn't question what Pat meant by her comment. In moments, they were at the dressing table, putting Liz's hair up in a tasteful French braid. She wore a minimum of makeup, so that didn't take long to do.

The knock at the door came just as they put the finishing touches on the exotic eye shadow that accentuated Liz's almond-shaped eyes.

Pat's anger returned with a passion, and she strode to the door and wrenched it open in a single, smooth motion. "You're late," she snapped at the uniformed driver.

The man checked his watch, blond brows lowering over deep blue eyes. He was no doubt accustomed to women falling at his feet, gauging by the calculated way he moved.

You're dealing with the wrong women tonight.

"No offense, ma'am. I was told the lady would be half an hour late. Was there an error?"

"Oh, there was an error all right." Pat ticked her finger his direction, handing a light jacket off to Liz with the other hand without looking her direction. "Luckily for you, you're not the one who made it."

* * * *

Pat's mood hadn't improved much by the time they reached the Fantasy Club. She was looking forward to a good old-fashioned verbal take-down, to watching some poor sap squirm in the face of her righteous fury.

"My God," Liz breathed.

Pat glanced toward the building, then leaned forward with a gasp of surprise. "I thought this would be one of the old plantations."

The driver chuckled. "It was, when Jupe bought it," he informed them. "The fields were gorgeous, but the manor was condemned. It wasn't a unique design, there were plenty of other plantations still standing, some as tourist attractions, and there was no historical significance to the site in particular, so the historical society had no problems with Jupe replacing it with something unique. The state certainly loved the idea of another paying establishment in the place of one up to its ears in hock. So, Jupe had the existing buildings leveled, cleared the fields to plant the gardens, and had the new building erected at the center."

It was the single most impressive structure Pat had ever seen. The Fantasy Club seemed to be constructed with marble, though common sense said costs would prohibit that. A series of columns graced the outer edge, creating a look not unlike the Parthenon. Large arched windows glowed with soft inner light, allowing Pat to note the three high stories and a glass dome on the roof.

"Jupe designed it all himself," the driver continued. "The gardens. The manor. Every detail. I suppose this place was *his* fantasy."

"Jupe?" Liz repeated, obviously as stunned as Pat was.

"Sorry, ma'am. Jack Jupiter. He's the owner of the club, the master magician of the house."

Pat smiled at that nugget of information. "Is he? Then Mr. Jupiter is the man I need to speak to." *By the time I'm through with him, he'll wish he could make* himself *disappear.*

The driver didn't answer that.

"It's fitting, isn't it?" Liz asked.

Pat met her gaze in confusion. "What is?"

She panned her gaze down Pat's body, then reached out and parted the long, light coat she had donned over her costume. "Your…um..."

"Costume." Pat nodded in understanding. "I suppose it is."

The costume sent for her was a dress the likes of which would have been seen on the statue of a Greek goddess. Comfortable sandals were strapped to her feet. A garland of live greens with tiny red flower buds encircled her head; the golden silk strands braided through it hung down her back and mingled with her hair. She hadn't given the costume much thought until now, but the only part of it that seemed odd was the silky gold bikini beneath the outer layer.

I'm sure the ancient Greeks didn't wear that.

Immaterial! Someone is playing a game with Liz, and that's unacceptable. I have to keep my head in that game, if I intend to win it. And Pat always made a point to win.

The car stopped at the base of a wide staircase that rose between two columns and ended at a huge pair of doors.

Pat winced at that. Liz hadn't brought her cane along, because they hadn't envisioned climbing so many stairs. Most businesses were handicapped accessible after all. Should they ask for the handicapped entrance? Before she could question Liz, her friend supplied an answer.

"I'll be fine. It's not like we're going to be here for long anyway."

The driver opened the door for them and offered his hand to Pat. She brushed it away and ducked from the car without his help, then ascended the first few stairs.

Liz refused his hand as well, but the driver placed it below her elbow, just in case she lost her balance. Pat tried not to find that commendable, but it was a lost cause. In the end, she admitted to herself it was a touching gesture.

"Well, we're here," Liz commented, as she stepped up beside her. "I suppose we should get climbing."

"Yes. Let's get this over with."

The house was larger than Pat first believed. *By far.* If the staircase was any indication, it was three times the size she'd estimated from a distance. "The ceilings have to be twenty feet high."

"These steps are marble," Liz offered.

"Impossible. Well, maybe marble facing, but blocks of marble this large would be too expensive."

She made an expansive arm movement. "Look at this place, Pat. Do you honestly think price was an issue for this Jupiter guy?"

"Jupe…please."

Pat snapped her head up, searching out the man leaning against a column in the moonlight. Like the voice, the man seemed to appear from nowhere. She backed off a step, nearly colliding with Liz in the process. "Where did you—?"

His laugh was rich and deep. "I do apologize. I was taking some air on the stairs"—he motioned absently—"in the shadow of the column. A break in the festivities, if you will.

"By the way, the ceilings are twenty-six feet high on all levels, save the dome, which is half that height at the outer edges. Yes. The stairs are marble. The entire manor is, where possible." His smile widened. "No expense was spared in building Little Olympus."

Pat realized she was staring, rapt on the golden-haired man before them. She shook herself mentally, annoyed that he'd managed to sidetrack her. She reclaimed her calm reserve, the aloof demeanor that made executives from competing companies sweat.

"You must be Mr. Jupiter," she noted.

"That I am. And you are undoubtedly Ms. Patrice Duberry and Ms. Elizabeth Reynolds. Welcome, ladies." He bowed to them. "Won't you come inside?"

There was something about his speech patterns and mannerisms that spoke of money or old-world education. *Or both.* Pat nodded and took the last six stairs nearly in time with Liz.

Inside, they handed off their coats to a staff member. Pat did her best to ignore the statues and fountains, gilded mirrors, and rushing servants in the uniform green and white. She had to stay focused on Jack Jupiter long enough to settle this matter as she'd promised Liz she would.

No matter how many distractions he throws in my way.

Jupiter motioned to the room around them. "At the Fantasy Club, we strive to offer the perfect evening to our guests."

"You screwed up this time," Pat informed him coolly.

His eyes widened. "A mistake? From *my* staff? I would be shocked."

She crossed her arms over her chest. "I assure you it's true."

"Everything is done to specifications. There are rigid controls in place to prevent—"

"Who checks these specifications? How do you assure that the person's requests—the one who arranges the invitation—aren't offensive to the invited guest?"

"Offensive?" He seemed genuinely scandalized by the suggestion. "What did you find offensive?"

Pat motioned to Liz. "Her costume—"

"Is lovely," Jupe noted. "You ladies find this gown offensive?"

Liz blanched, and tears formed in her eyes.

"Of course not!" Pat reined in her frustration a notch. *Never let your opponent know he's gotten to you.* "This isn't the costume you sent. There was no way—"

"It's not?" The note of horror in his tone was impossible to miss.

"No. The costume *your*—"

"Oh, this is highly irregular. The invitation clearly—"

"Mr. Jupiter, that costume was in such poor taste—"

"Problem, Jupe?"

Pat turned on the interloper, intent on telling him to butt out. The words caught in her throat. No. The breath caught in her lungs. Pat reminded herself to cycle her breath in and out. That didn't help. It brought with it scents of heat and musk.

"Ah, Eric." Jupe sighed in what sounded like relief. "Patrice Duberry, meet Eric Valentine, my event coordinator. Eric, Ms. Duberry has a problem with your costume choice for Ms. Reynolds. Would you be kind enough to handle this while I greet guests?"

Valentine didn't smile. His blue eyes were locked with Pat's, intense, serious. "Absolutely. If you would come with me, Patrice?"

"Of course." The words were out without consideration. They sounded strange in her own ears, as if someone else had spoken them. *Did he call me Patrice?* It should have offended her, if he had, but it didn't.

"If you'll come with me, Ms. Reynolds?" Jupe requested.

"Pat?" There was a slight note of unease in Liz's question.

Valentine leaned slightly closer. "There's no reason for her to miss the festivities for mundane business." His whisper puffed over her lips, sending an odd tremor through her stomach.

But I promised Liz.

"There are quite a few stairs. She won't be comfortable climbing them."

A pang of regret she couldn't trace the origins of struck Pat hard in the chest. "Go ahead, Liz. I'll...catch up soon."

A smile curved the edge of Valentine's mouth. He turned away abruptly, leaving Pat reeling. "Right this way," he instructed, oblivious to her upset.

Pat followed closely behind, taking the time to examine him as they mounted the marble staircase tucked into an alcove with glass walls overlooking the dark gardens.

Valentine's hair was a mass of white-blond curls, left loose around his face, not tamed and pulled back in a ponytail, as Jupiter wore his darker hair. Muscular but not muscle bound, his skin was smooth and darkly tan.

Maybe not tan? It almost looks as if he has naturally olive-toned skin.

She gasped in the realization that he was wearing a short, belted tunic, edged in gold.

Roman style? Or was that Greek? The Romans and Greeks passed so much back and forth, including the Greek gods, it was hard to keep track of which was which.

And does it really matter?

It didn't. It also didn't matter that the sight of him in it was beyond aesthetically pleasing. It was a new sensation, one Pat really didn't need to deal with while she still had a score to settle with this man.

Pat gave up on trying to size up the competition. There was something about the men who ran this club that defied definition. She prepared herself for the coming confrontation, but nothing could have prepared her for where Valentine led her.

The dome was huge. Beneath it, the space was separated only by planting beds of all forms of foliage. She could make out flowering bushes close to her, but there appeared to be fruit-bearing trees further in.

The portion of the room closest to the door appeared to be an office, though—further in—Pat could make out what looked like a formal dining room and a sunken tub of some sort.

The air was humid and heavy in the perfume of living greenery.

"What is this place?" she asked.

"My home...and my office." Valentine rifled through what appeared to be a wide oak filing cabinet. "You know, the Japanese have found that workers are happier and healthier, both physically and emotionally, when they have natural light and live plants in the workspace."

She gaped at him. "Home? You live here?" That took the idea of living in an apartment over the store to a whole new level.

"Yes. I do. Jupe built the dome with me in mind. I could hardly say 'no' to his job offer, with this perk as part of the package."

"That's quite a job offer." She looked up at the top of the dome, a dizzying height overhead.

"Apparently, he felt I was worth the expense to keep me on the grounds." The comment was self-effacing, delivered without a hint of hubris that said he knew he was worth it.

She wasn't sure whether she should trust his seeming modesty. Instead, Pat moved the discussion to a neutral topic. "It must get awfully bright during the day."

"Not at all. Portions of the dome are light reactive. They shade the working and sleeping areas for me."

"The plants were chosen accordingly?"

"Hmmm? Oh, yes. They were." He motioned a hand at the dome absently. "There are also automated vent systems to equalize temperature and to allow air flow, and the dome uses the latest clear solar cell technology. It powers the entire estate area."

"Quite an undertaking," she noted. "Light reactive glass in panes that large..." Pat couldn't even estimate the cost of something like that.

"Yes. The manor...the entire estate is a marvel." His tone didn't make it seem as if he viewed it as a marvel. On the contrary, he sounded bored.

Stars burned and winked in the darkness beyond the dome. "How could anyone get bored with this view?" she mused.

"Beg your pardon?"

"Hmmm?" The stars were so clear and bright, Pat felt she could reach out and touch them.

"Ms. Duberry?"

Pat gasped in the abrupt realization of how lost she'd been; she pasted on her game face again. "Yes. Of course. It is a spectacular view." She turned back to the desk, intent on her professional best.

The best laid plans of mice and men. She'd surely seen men as gorgeous as Eric Valentine before.

Oh...really?

Pat forced herself not to wince. He looked even better from the front than he looked from the back. How was she supposed to concentrate with him in the room?

Nowhere was safe to look. His eyes disarmed her. His mouth made her wish for things she'd thought she'd stopped hoping for long ago. His arms were strong and lightly dusted with the same barely darker than platinum hair that curled around his face. Pat licked her lower lip, wondering if his chest was as well.

"Yes," he commented.

Pat snapped a startled look at his face. Had he read her mind or something? "Yes, what?" she demanded.

Valentine ran his gaze down her body. "The view. Truly spectacular. You were born to wear a dress like that. Even I didn't realize how well it would suit you. I am quite impressed."

She crossed her arms over her chest, as her nipples came to points against the soft fabric. "Don't try it. I'm immune to flattery. Now, back to the mistake your office made." *Damned infuriating man.*

His eyes hardened ever so slightly. "I assure you, Patrice… May I call you Patrice?"

I guess he didn't call me that earlier. Why did that sting? "Pat," she answered automatically. She clamped her mouth shut, horrified with herself. *What am I doing?* She'd never invited a business associate, let alone a competitor, to call her anything but Duberry or Ms. Duberry.

Valentine shook his head. "Pat is a boy's name. Patty is for little girls. Patrice is a woman's name."

She nodded. Patrice was certainly more acceptable than Pat was. It was formal; it would provide a separation between them that calling her Pat wouldn't. *Now that I've invited him to call me Pat, it's the best I've got.*

"Very well. I assure you, Patrice…" He paused, as if gauging the effect of the name on her.

Pat shivered in pleasure. It made no sense. She'd always hated the name Patrice, but something about the timbre of Eric's voice when he said it made it seem she'd never heard her own name before.

Eric? No. He's not Eric. He's Valentine!

"…that there was no mistake."

The spell was broken with a nearly audible snap. "What? You sent that costume on *purpose*? You sent Liz—"

"A wedding dress. Yes. That was no mistake."

Pat leaned toward him across the desk, abandoning the shield across her chest to slam her hands on the desktop between them. "I want the name," she demanded.

"Name?"

"The name of the person who ordered this. Someone has used you to concoct a very expensive, elaborate, and cruel prank. I'm sure you'll want to cooperate with making the culprit pay for it."

Valentine sighed. "I'm afraid I can't do that."

"What? Why not?" Pat realized there was no file on the desk between them. *What was he doing in the cabinet? Wasting time?*

"There are two reasons. The first is the confidentiality pact between us and our clients."

"I'll file charges. You can be forced to open your files." Was that what he wanted? He couldn't be sued, if he was forced to reveal the information.

"That will only be effective if you can prove malicious intent on the part of the client. I cannot help you, because there was no malicious intent."

Pat gasped for breath, stunned. "How can you… Are you dense? Do you do any…?"

"Background checks? Of course. On the client and on the invited guest. I realize—from your point of view—it must have seemed a horrible choice to—"

"Seemed? You crass—" Pat struggled for the words to calmly explain her point. *Fuck this.* "Liz was in tears, you jerk! Don't you get it?"

Something that looked remarkably like remorse flashed in his expression. He hid it almost before she noted it. "I know. I could see it on her when she arrived."

"And you still feel this was a good idea?" she challenged.

"Yes. I do. Liz was wearing the dress she wore when Ben asked her to marry him."

"How could you know that?" Who were they getting their information from? To her knowledge, neither Karen nor Jane would remember that fact, if they ever knew it.

"Our information is flawless," he offered in a wry tone. "Look..." Valentine sighed. "If Liz could find closure... If she could find a way not to wake every morning, riddled by emotional trauma she cannot escape, would you support that?" His expression said he was sincere, perhaps even hopeful he could deliver that. "Would you, Patrice?"

"I... You know I would, but how is opening old wounds going to accomplish anything productive?"

"Would you have believed she would ever wear that dress again until she did?"

"No, but what does that have to do with anything?" Pat asked, off balance by all the sudden jumps in logic.

"Liz had that dress...and all the other dresses that reminded her of Ben packed away in the back of her closet. In the same way, she carries all the pain in the back of her mind, coloring everything she sees, hears, and does. As long as she's living the past every day, locking away every memory that way, she can never find peace."

That was hard to argue, but years of therapy hadn't changed that. What was Valentine and Company going to do in a single night to change it?

"You want something from me. That's why you brought me here to talk to me." Pat didn't question it.

"Let Liz find her way to peace alone. Don't interfere. Don't even join her downstairs."

A potent silence fell between them. Pat used it to take a second look at the situation. "You used me to get her here? You knew she wouldn't come unless she thought she had me as her…?"

"Shield, more or less." He didn't deny it.

"I have your word that this will help Liz and not leave her hurting worse than she already is?"

"Yes. It is my aim to provide that for her. You have my absolute assurances of it."

She considered that, torn. "If this goes wrong, I will get the best lawyers in Virginia for Liz."

A smile touched his lips. "Understood."

"Fine. If you would call me a car—" Pat faltered, taken in by the near-panic in Valentine's eyes. "What is it?"

"Dinner," he rasped.

"What?" What was he asking? Or offering?

"I took the liberty of arranging dinner. Would you join me?"

Pat tried to sort her feelings on the matter. She didn't completely trust Eric Valentine. *I don't trust anyone at* the Fantasy Club. It wasn't wise to split her allegiances. Still, she wouldn't mind getting to know Valentine better. *Maybe, if I spend time with him, I'll figure out why he rattles me.*

"Patrice?"

She startled. Valentine was beside her, in her personal space. Pat met his gaze, feeling the now-familiar punch of simmering emotions that descended when he was this close to her.

"Patrice?"

What did he ask? "Yes?"

"Dinner? Will you join me?"

"Of course." *Was there any question?*

Chapter Four

Eros smiled. He stepped back from her, allowing Patrice's mind to clear slightly. As he expected, the pained expression heralding her confusion contorted her face again.

"I should stay, in case Liz needs me," she blurted out.

He reined in his frustration with her attempts to save face and explain herself. *She's agreed to dinner. It's a start.* Eros notified Jupe by their mind link of his requirements for the meal, mindful of keeping up the ruse that he'd already ordered said meal.

The discord in the manor grated at his already-taxed nerves, and Eros blocked as much of it as he could. Jupe would put out the flash-fires, for now. The best way Eros had to aid him… The *only* way to aid him was continuing down the path with Patrice.

It would take time for Patrice to accept what she was born to be. The last time Eros took a consort, women were still identified at birth and trained for the position. The idea of being soul-bound with a god hadn't frightened her predecessors. He'd never faced the possibility of failure before.

Patrice smoothed her fiery hair, looking to the dome again. "It really is gorgeous." She shot a nervous look at him out of the corner of her eye.

The moment earlier, when she'd shown her passion for the view, had let him know the plans for this dome had been sound. Of course, those plans had been made much earlier in her life, before he was suffering fully from the loss of his last consort.

"Would you like to see it to its best advantage?" he offered.

"How?"

She glanced around, as if searching for a door to the surrounding roof. There was one, but that wasn't what Eros had in mind.

"If you would allow me to darken the lights, you'll have a much better view of the stars."

She flushed slightly. He could tell she was questioning his motives.

"I will light candles, of course—if you wish. We just need to extinguish the artificial light under the dome."

Patrice nodded. "That would be excellent. It's a unique opportunity to see the stars this way."

It doesn't have to be. Eros tipped his head, then made his way to the dining area. Once the candelabra was lit, he collected a spare duvet and silk pillow from the linen cabinet, then spread them out on the strip of grass between the dining area and the bar.

She eyed it suspiciously. "And that is for?" she prompted him.

"You. I will get the lights. Would you care for a drink while we wait for dinner?"

"Red wine?"

He smiled wider. "As you wish. I have just the vintage." With that, he left her behind and turned off the overhead lights. He pretended to use a remote, but—truth be told—he had no need of anything so mundane.

Eros retrieved a decorative bottle from shelves behind the bar then pulled down two glasses. He savored the scent of Bacchus's best vintage. His consort deserved no less than the best.

Not the magical version, of course. It wouldn't do to trick Patrice into accepting him.

He'd known she would want red wine. Eros always knew his consorts, their likes and dislikes, their most intimate desires. Patrice had refined tastes. It wouldn't be Egyptian beer or gladiatorial fights for this consort.

Wine and glasses in hand, Eros returned to her side. Patrice seemed oblivious to him, lost in her examination of the depths of space outside the dome. She shivered as he drew near, and his cock erupted in a maddening throbbing for her.

He avoided touching her, knowing what that first brush of skin on skin would do to them both. It was too soon for that. The burn would frighten her. As soon as Patrice took the full glass from his hand, Eros retreated to the table.

Dinner first, he soothed himself. *After that, I will introduce Patrice to what she is.*

Eros could force her compliance. He could bind her to him unknowing, but it wasn't in his nature to do so. As much as it pained him to do it, he'd rather pay the price of failure written in the stars—a thousand years of loneliness, during which war would reign—than take an unwilling consort.

"Mmmm."

Her rumble of pleasure sent fingers of anticipation down his spine. Eros sipped his wine, needing the calming effect. *I've tarried too long.* He'd waited a decade and a half beyond the time it would be considered appropriate to claim her as his own. Patrice was a full decade older than any other consort he'd bound to him.

As a result, his power was waning, worse than even Jupe suspected. In truth, if Eros didn't claim Patrice tonight, the Fantasy Club might suffer the first failures in its long, proud history.

"This is wonderful," Patrice murmured.

Eros chanced a look at her. Patrice was a picture of sensuality, laid out as if inviting him to devour her. Her lips were slightly parted, her color high, her eyes half-closed in languid repose.

Patrice unconsciously invited his attention. She traced the edge of the crystal with her fingertip. Her back was arched ever so slightly; the points of her nipples stood out against the folds of fabric that covered them. Her legs were spread just enough that she wouldn't be stimulating the aroused flesh between them. Her scent permeated the air between them, a sweet perfume that pleaded for his touch.

She took another drink of the wine, the burgundy liquid sliding along plump lips and a tongue that—

He snapped his gaze away, reining in his control. "Would you like more?" he offered.

Patrice chuckled, a husky sound that gripped Eros at the base of his cock. He bit back a groan. He'd waited far too long this time.

"Are you trying to get me drunk?" she teased.

Eros closed his eyes, tempted to do just that. *It would be taking advantage.* "Maybe you should wait for dinner." *The torture of Ixion! Why am I doing this to myself?*

She laughed harder. "Don't be silly."

He opened his eyes, his gaze locking on her raised hand— on the wine glass tipping back and forth between her thumb and forefinger. Eros tried to ignore the jut of her breasts, the pout of her lips. He failed. He found himself moving, crossing the distance between them, longing for the first touch.

A loud knock brought him back to his senses. *What am I doing?* Eros jerked his hand back and turned on his heel, then headed for the door. "Dinner," he grumbled. "Be right back."

He opened the door, furious with himself, expecting one of the many employees on the other side. Eros startled, meeting Jupe's hard look straight-on.

"Why didn't you tell me?" Jupe demanded in a fierce whisper.

"Your guests—"

"How do you think I knew? Your power is waning. You should have warned me."

Eros nodded. "I will convince her." *But I've never had to convince a consort before.* How did one *convince* a woman to embrace a life she never wanted, never knew she was destined to, with a man she's barely met?

Jupe grimaced, no doubt reading the thought clearly in Eros's diminished state. "Do it. You know the penalty."

"Mr. Valentine?"

Both men turned to look at her. Patrice stood beneath a lemon tree, her shoulder pressed to the thin trunk, the wine glass dangling from her fingertips, and her head cocked to one side. Eros forced a calming breath.

"Hello, Mr. Jupiter," she drawled.

The lilt of her slight accent played at his tenuous control.

Jupe pushed the food cart at Eros, demanding his attention. When he had it, Jupe sent his mental command to Eros.

She is yours. She wants you. Take her and be done with it. Then he was gone, closing the door behind him and striding toward the small service elevator.

Take her? It's a damned good thing my power doesn't rest in your hands, Jupiter. Of course, they already knew that. There was a reason he'd roped Jupe into operating the club with him. *One day, I will teach Jupiter what true love is.*

As Eros expected, Jupe pretended this particular discussion wasn't happening, though Eros made sure he heard it.

* * * *

Pat sipped at the wine, watching Valentine out of the corner of her eyes. "So, Mr. Valentine—"

"Eric," he corrected her.

"Eric, then." He was already calling her Patrice. "I don't suppose you're going to tell me which of my friends told you I like prime rib, salmon, stuffed mushrooms—"

He laughed heartily, his blue eyes glittering in what looked suspiciously like glee. "I don't think I will."

"Don't worry. I'll find out," she promised.

"Will you?" It was clearly a challenge.

Pat had never been one to pass up on a challenge. "I will. I have some concept of what this escapade costs. I've seen the reviews."

His smile dimmed somewhat. "It won't work."

"Come now. Charge card or bank account... Someone I know very well arranged for and paid for this."

"Yes and no." He drank down some of his wine, seemingly considering his words carefully.

"Excuse me?" What did that mean?

Eric leaned back, watching the stars. "Those who pay bring in more than enough money for us to take...appeals for our help. We don't advertise it, of course. The demand would be phenomenal, but those who need us seem to find us. Word of mouth, I suppose."

Pat shook her head in disbelief. "Are you telling me Liz is a charity case to you?"

He raised his head. It was an agonizing moment before he answered. "Not in the way you think," he assured her. "We never devalue our work. Every client and guest gets our best effort, whether they pay dearly for it or not at all. Look around, Patrice. Do you think a bit of pro bono work bothers us? Destroys our profit margin?"

She glanced around at the tropical plants, set under what felt like the gates of heaven. "I see your point."

"Fancy a soak?"

Pat furrowed her brow, her attention riveted to a strange-flowering bush covered in tight red buds. She touched the circlet of flowers in her hair. They were the same. Weren't they?

"Patrice?"

"What?"

"The hot tub? You did wear the gold swimsuit under your gown, didn't you?"

She gasped in the realization that Eric knew every stitch of clothing on her body.

He smiled widely. "If you didn't, I can order up another from—"

"I did," she admitted.

"Good. There's nothing like a soak to unwind after a filling meal. Care to join me?" Eric rose without waiting for an answer. He strode into the darkness toward the back of the dome.

Soft illumination came from the floor twenty feet or so away, outlining Eric's form. The sound of bubbling water broke the stillness, and the perfume of salt and lavender overwhelmed the smell of growth.

Eric crouched and untied his sandals. He set them aside and stood. After a moment of movement, his sash slid to the floor. Pat swallowed hard, the question of what was under the tunic making her dizzy. Before she could find the air or voice to ask that question, he'd pulled the garment off over his head and revealed what she suspected was a gold Speedo.

Pat's breathing hitched, and she was abruptly glad for the sound of churning water. She ran a shaking hand through her hair as Eric stepped into the pool.

What was it about him? She'd never been particularly fascinated by men. For a short time, other high school girls had decided she was a lesbian. After all, no *normal* teenage girl could be immune to Brad Jacobs.

Even then, Pat had known they were wrong. She wasn't gay. She couldn't be, because she had no more interest in women than she had in men.

Still, something had to be done to counter the rumor mill. So, when Brad had asked Pat to the Junior year spring dance, she'd ground her teeth and accepted. All in all, the night had been uninspired. Pat had felt nothing but a vague interest and pain with everything Brad did, even when she gave him her virginity.

She'd tried to convince herself that it was a combination of nerves and inexperience—perhaps the clumsy boy she'd had for a sexual partner—but the next four experiences had showed no change in Pat's reactions. She'd learned to go through the motions: kissing, petting, moving in tandem, but saying she found the whole thing strangely devoid of any real emotion or sensation—positive or negative—would be highly accurate.

Pat panned her gaze over Eric again. *Until now.* Eric hadn't even touched her, and her body ached in need. Her typically damp core was drenched, and her nipples hadn't gone down since the first time he'd raked his gaze up and down her body. *The same nipples that stayed flat when nearly half a dozen other men showered them with attention.*

Worse, her mind was making up for all those years of wondering what other girls thought when they looked at Brad. Visions of touching Eric's chest, stroking her hand up his cock, feeling his fingers filling her, his mouth—

"Patrice? Are you coming?"

She met his gaze, her errant body screaming for him. *Nearly coming, standing right here. But not nearly close enough.*

"I don't bite," he teased. "If it makes you feel better, I'll stay across the tub from you."

Her face heated. *What kind of fool am I? As if Eric wants me? The man hasn't even touched me. If it wasn't his job to keep me out of the way, he'd probably be off with—*

"Patrice, are you all right?"

"I should probably go. You must have better things to do than—"

"Get in the tub, Patrice."

She was moving toward him, shedding clothing onto the floor, without the slightest hesitation, without any qualms about the fact that she'd just followed his orders. Pat wasn't the type of woman who followed a man's orders.

When the hot water started lapping at her chest, some semblance of sanity seeped back into her mind. Pat looked around at the clothing strewn across the room in confusion.

She met Eric's gaze. "Why are you different?" Pat clapped a hand over her mouth. Why did she lack common sense when he was nearby? Where had her ability to censor herself gone?

Eric didn't react to that. "Different?"

Pat eased the hand away from her mouth, nodding sheepishly. "From other men." *In for a penny, in for a pound.*

"Ah. I wondered when we would get to this." A wry smile pulled up at one side of his lips.

His tone irritated her. "To what?"

"Why aren't you *immune* to me, as you thought you were all these years? Like you have been with other men?"

Pat felt the color drain from her face. "They wouldn't dare! How…would they…?"

"No. Your friends could hardly tell me what you've never confided in them. Though you've told Liz that you're asexual, you've never admitted to anyone that you've been frigid so far."

She winced at the word. There it was. She was defective, just as the other girls claimed she was.

Eric scowled and continued. "But you're not frigid, and you know that now. You're not asexual either. Your problem was the partners you chose. You are a woman who was born for a single man. No other man will do for you."

"What?" Her voice came out as a hoarse croak.

"You could leave this room and find any other man downstairs. This anticipation would fade, and you would feel nothing. If I touch you—" His eyes darkened, making her heart race.

"Y-yes?" *Why am I asking this? What could really happen from a touch?*

"The release of your bottled sexual energy would roll through you like a tsunami," he promised, his expression serious and solemn.

"From a touch?" she scoffed.

Eric nodded. "A single touch. Not even a sexual touch."

Pat planted her fists on her hips. "You are seriously disturbed, Mr. Valentine."

"Eros," he corrected her.

"What?" Her mind spun. "Oh, I get it. Ha ha ha. I suppose no one told you, but Jupiter is Roman, and Eros is Greek. Olympus is Greek, too. You guys are mixing your pantheons."

"Jupe prefers the Roman name for him. I prefer the Greek. Since the Romans adopted everyone else's gods, and they gave us due worship, which names we choose to use is hardly of any concern."

"So you're telling me you're the *real* Eros? God of sexual fantasies and all that?"

"God of love and lust," he countered.

She turned to leave, grumbling curses.

"Prove me wrong," he offered.

Pat shot him a glare. "How?"

"Well, you could touch me and prove you don't climax just from contact with me."

"Safe bet," she grumbled. "Or? I hear another suggestion couched in that."

His expression went hard in challenge. "Or go fuck one of the men downstairs and see how fast your body forgets these lovely feelings."

Pat stared at him, outraged at his crass suggestion. *I should. It would serve him right if I—*

"If that's your choice, go ahead. Test all you want. I have all night."

Something dark and dangerous reared up in her. *How dare he.* Pat launched at him and slapped him hard across the face.

Her balance deserted her, and she fell against his chest. Pat stiffened as his arms closed around her—not in fury but rather in overpowering pleasure. Her body trembled uncontrollably, sparks of pleasure echoing through her breasts, womb, and thighs until waves of searing heat coursed over her nerves.

Pat screamed, a multitude of alien sensations warring for supremacy. A throbbing built inside her, intensifying, accentuating an emptiness she needed Eric to fill.

His mouth closed over hers, his tongue dancing a frantic dance she'd learned to mimic. Pat knew the steps, but she'd never felt the passion and drive. *Until now.*

Eric held her head tight to his with one hand, his tongue exploring her, inviting hers to play. He stroked his other hand in patterns down the length of her spine.

Pat pressed her body to his in response, a surge of power drowning out the waning climax. She'd always wondered what other women felt, whether or not they actually felt those fantastic things they talked about in excited whispers.

Eric's mouth left hers. He stroked his lips along the line of her jaw, then nibbled on her ear. "I'm sorry," he whispered. "I shouldn't have said it. I should have let you decide for yourself."

"You would have—" Pat groaned at the heavy ridge teasing her stomach.

"Yes. I should have let you try another male, if that was your wish. I couldn't. I've waited too long for you to let you take someone else as a test." Eric ran his hands down her back; he cupped Pat's buttocks and lifted her. He closed his spread legs and set her astride them.

Visions of herself impaled on him stole her breath. Pat wriggled closer to Eric, riding the line of his cock through his suit. "Please," she managed, her lips trembling.

* * * *

Eros groaned, wishing he could take her now, but there were forms to be observed. Patrice had to know what was happening, what she was accepting.

Patrice eased her hips back and forth, stimulating them both with the near-perfect contact of their bodies. He forced his mind back to his purpose, then moaned as she licked at one of his nipples. If she continued, he would toss out the formalities like so much waste. He had to take charge.

Eros eased her hips away from his, capturing her protest in a heated kiss as she raised her head. A shared rumbling of satisfaction teased his senses as Eros slipped his fingers past her bikini bottoms and plunged two inside her.

She stopped moving abruptly, his fingers buried to the hilt inside her. Patrice looked up at him, as he eased out of the kiss. He played his fingers inside her, holding her back by her shoulder when she would have sought out his mouth again.

"Eric?" Her voice was a husky whisper.

"Eros," he corrected her.

"Oh...God!" It was a plea for understanding, an expression of her body's reach for another climax, and her manner of begging for the one thing he had to deny her.

For now.

A chuckle burst from his chest at her choice of words. "One of them," he agreed pleasantly.

"Jupiter. Shit, I met—" She closed her eyes, tipping her hips to capture more of his fingers.

A stab of jealousy made Eros grumble. *Never.* Another man's name would never pass her lips while he made love to her. *Certainly not the name of that lowly dog, Jupiter.* The need to reinforce that rode him hard.

"Look at me, Patrice." He allowed his fierce determination to color the demand.

Patrice opened her eyes wide in confusion.

"Who am I? Say my name." *Step one. Accept me as I am.*

She hesitated, uncertain, a touch of fear burning in her eyes.

"Say my name. Not as a sex game. Say it and believe it."

"Er-Eros."

He nodded, offering her a smile in the attempt to calm her. "What do you want, Patrice?"

Her gaze left his, straying down his chest to the bulge of his cock, though it had to be barely visible through the sluggish swirl of lighted water flowing between their bodies. The cockhead peeked from the top of his swimsuit, and he wondered if Patrice could see it.

As if in answer, she reached for it.

"No."

She jerked her hand back minutely, inches from her goal.

"Not yet," he soothed her. He turned the fingers within her, stoking Patrice deeper.

"How can you do this for me?"

"Who am I?"

"Eros." There was no hesitation.

"Look at me."

Patrice met his gaze.

"You believe who I am?"

"Yes."

Thank all the gods! He smiled. "You spoke the truth. I know you did, because we are incapable of lying to each other, now that we've touched."

She started to speak, then faltered. A deep blush darkened her skin to nearly the color of her hair.

"Ask me. Ask me anything."

"Will you—leave me when the night is over? Will I—" She dropped her gaze to his chest, biting back a sob.

Eros cupped her chin, noting the confident mask she had donned. *Saving face.* "No. I would never let you suffer the loss. If you'll have me, of course."

"H-have?" She gasped, her body reaching for another climax.

He eased off, letting Patrice burn but not willing to store more of her released passion. *Not while I need my wits about me to convince her.* Eros considered his answer carefully, rejecting the ways he'd *planned* to explain it to her.

"I am the god of love and lust," he began solemnly.

Patrice shot him a hungry look.

Step two, he reminded himself. *Accept what* you *are.* "The god of love and lust is bound to his state. By that, I mean that I require a consort."

"A mistress?" she asked.

"A companion. A lover." He smiled. "A wife." Eros ducked his head, sucking the tip of one breast…then the other.

Patrice grasped at his shoulder, using him for balance. "Why me?" she questioned, her words measured.

He straightened. "Remove the top. I want to see your breasts."

"Eros," she warned.

He chuckled darkly. None of his former consorts had dared challenge him. *None of them ever believed it was their choice whether or not to be bound to me. It was their fate. They were raised to believe that. To know it as fact.*

A niggling of unease swept through him. The consorts had been raised to know their place, and Eros had approached them as if there were no question that they would join with him, as was ordained. Perhaps that was why they always lost interest over the centuries with him.

"Eros?" Concern laced her voice.

"When a consort tires of me, she can choose to embrace death."

"But, why—?"

"When that happens," he spoke over her, "another is born. For a time, I am alone. Long ago, these consorts were raised with my priests and trained to be my consort. I came for them when they matured." *And acted as if it was my* right *to have them, as Jupe acted as if Patrice was mine to take. Have I been that blind?*

"But I wasn't raised that way. I had no idea… Am I really…?" Confusion clouded her lovely green eyes.

"You are. The religions have ranged too far. Your mother surely knew you had a destiny, but she wouldn't have known what the destiny was. Even if she sought out one of the so-called practitioners of the old faith, it would be highly unlikely the fool would have correctly identified your purpose."

Patrice nodded solemnly. "My mother always said I was born for a purpose. I just never expected..." She motioned in an indiscriminate little circle, expressing her uncertainty clearly.

Eros nodded. If she chose not to become his consort, the energy of her releases would see Jupe's guests through the night, but there would be no more power for a millennium.

She was silent for a moment, seemingly lost deep in thought. Then Patrice reached behind her back and released the bows holding the gold cups over her breasts.

Eros suckled at the tip of one perfect breast before the bikini top had a chance to float to the far reaches of the tub. He nibbled his way up her chest and throat, anticipating the wave of climax coming.

Come on. Let's finish step two. "Look at the flowers, Patrice."

She turned her head, focusing on one of the bushes of buds surrounding the tub and the bed at the center of the dome. "Beautiful," she murmured.

"They are Love Blooms, my personal flower. Watch them."

He drove her over again, his cock aching at the need to join her. Eros drew in her passion, reeling at her potency. He let just a little escape his grasp, just enough to cause the flowers to react.

And maybe enough to set off some of the more sensitive lovers in the crowd.

The tight buds spread to reveal tantalizing peeks at the metallic gold shimmering inside. Patrice gasped, reaching a hand out to touch the nearest blossom. "They're opening," she breathed.

"Only halfway for now," he admitted. If she became his consort, they would open fully. If she refused him, the Love Blooms would wither and die, as would his power. For a full millennium, the bushes would be blackened bushes of thorns, bearing neither flowers nor leaves, but not quite dead. They would be cold and barren, inhospitable. *As useless as my powers will be.*

Eros reveled in the fluttering of her inner muscles around his fingers.

Patrice met his gaze solidly. "Make them open," she begged.

He traced the fingers of his free hand over her lips, then down her chin. "I cannot. These flowers only respond to you." *As does my magic.* "If you agree to be my mate, they will open fully. When they begin to wilt—" He swallowed hard at that. Every time he saw the flowers darken, the petals pull in on themselves, it meant his consort had chosen to embrace death. Eros felt true fear when that happened, despair, madness. Those were the worst moments of his long life.

Pain settled in her expression. "Why do they choose to leave you?" she asked, as if the concept stunned her.

"Perhaps..." Eros found his mind making leaps of logic that disturbed him. He eased his fingers out of her body; it seemed disloyal to his current consort to fixate so avidly on his interactions with earlier consorts while he was arousing her.

The inspection didn't relieve the ache in his gut. Why had he never questioned this before? "Perhaps sexual satisfaction is not enough," he whispered.

"Is that all you offer?"

"No. Of course not." He had given his consorts everything they wanted or needed. He had doted on them, but had he ever let them see how much he needed them? *Never.* It had never seemed important to do so. Eros was a god. His sense of pride demanded that he act his place, that he be aloof to such concerns. *Or at least that I hide any weaknesses.*

Did women long for that? Would knowing he wasn't invulnerable fulfill some need in them? Eros suffered greatly without a consort, and he reveled in the touch of one, but he'd always felt admitting that mundane, beneath him. His consorts were human women. Perhaps they needed to know more of the man and less of the god.

Eros looked to Patrice, suddenly fearful. He'd never wanted to give a consort that much power over him. He'd never wanted a consort to know her leaving would crush him. Though he told them how special they were, what had Eros shared with them of himself that would convince them one was different to him than another? That she wasn't simply a new face and willing body, there for him to use until she tired of him?

Love is built on trust, he reminded himself. Eros had never trusted his heart fully to a consort. *By doing so, I made a mockery of their purpose—and mine. Without trust, love does not exist, and it was naught but lust and infatuation we shared.*

"What is it?" Patrice interrupted his self-recrimination.

"Ask me anything," Eros offered. "I want you to know me. I want..." *What I have obviously never known before.* That realization hurt. "I want you to choose to stay with me. I don't want to lose you."

Her eyes widened in what was likely surprise. "What does being your consort mean?"

Not the same as it did with any of the others. He would make sure of that. "It is different with each consort. We must forge our own agreement of what constitutes our union."

"That doesn't tell me much," she noted. "How long do your consorts usually choose to stay with you?"

Eros shrugged uncomfortably. "Arene chose to leave me after only a century. Chloe chose to stay with me for almost a millennium. Nine hundred and seventy-two years, to be precise."

"A-a century? Millennium? You mean your consort could be immortal, if she wanted to be?"

"If she wants to be my consort that long…of course," he confirmed. "She is both ageless and immortal, until she chooses to embrace death."

There was a moment of silence between them. "What happens if you get tired of her and don't want her as your consort anymore?"

He struggled to form words in his shock. "Tire of a consort? While she lives, a consort is the whole of my existence. When one chooses death, a piece of me dies with her. I-I suppose that's why I chose not to seek you out for so long. After Chloe… I thought she might choose to stay forever. When five centuries passed…then six…"

One crimson eyebrow went up in a look of speculation. "You're not one of those demanding husbands who want to order every…?"

"Patrice," he exclaimed, mortified at what she was suggesting.

She shot him what he didn't doubt was a mock-innocent and slightly-apologetic look. "Well, you *are* male—and a god—and…" Patrice sighed.

"And?" he challenged, caught between amusement and exasperation with her.

Her gaze strayed to his pulsing cock. "No doubt very good at convincing women to whatever you want."

"Do you want me to convince you, Patrice?" Eros stroked a hand down his length, smiling as her body called to him.

"Yes," she admitted.

"As my consort wishes."

Chapter Five

Pat shivered in anticipation, watching Eros stroke himself again. And again. She licked her lower lip, wondering what sucking that cock would feel like. Would it arouse her? It never had before—not that men seemed to care if she got anything out of it, as long as she made sure they had a good time.

She ranged her gaze up and down his body. Yes. There was little doubt that sucking Eros would be a very different experience.

A fine shudder passed through him. Eros nodded, resolute, his expression potent. He slid his hands down her hips and cupped Pat's buttocks in his palms. Eros stood, cradling her to his body, stepped from the hot tub, then strode further into the dome.

He settled her on her feet beside a huge bed, wider and longer than king size.

"God size." She giggled at that; it sounded odd coming from her own throat. She wasn't a giggling type. *Until now?*

Eros hooked the gold bikini bottom and eased it down her hips. He uncovered the scarlet curls beneath, hesitated for a moment, seemingly rapt on the view, then growled in appreciation.

Pat gasped as he dropped to his knees, nuzzling at her curls as he pulled the suit off. He urged her to raise one foot, then the other, to accomplish the task.

Eros shouldered her legs further apart, then hooked his shoulders behind her knees and lifted. She fell back on the silk, sliding as Eros guided her further onto the mattress, leaving everything below her lower back off the edge, supported by his broad shoulders.

His breath on her was the only warning Pat had before Eros's tongue feathered over her clit. She cried out softly in response. She'd thought women made up the stories about being eaten out, but it was even more intense than they'd said it was. Or maybe it was because it was Eros's mouth on her.

He explored her core slowly, tracing the seam and flicking his tongue inside, pressing the flat to her, circling her clit. He sucked in the aching nub, ruthlessly introducing her to the pleasure only he could give her.

He eased away slightly. "Convincing you," he breathed.

Pat wanted to ask what he meant, but his mouth heating her nether lips and his tongue swirling inside her scattered her thinking mind. Her body exploded in a fierce hunger. She needed his cock buried in her. She craved it like she'd never craved anything before.

"Now, Eros," she begged. "I need you."

His tongue retreated, and his fingers trailed up and down her slit. Pat cried out harshly, aching and frustrated.

"This is the final step, Patrice. I cannot give you what you seek unless you agree to be my consort. You can take what I offer for hours, one shattering orgasm after another to my mouth and hands, but if I climax in your body, it seals our union."

She licked her lips, considering that. Was she ready to trade her freedom and independence? *What am I trading it for? Immortality and eternal youth, for as long as I choose it. Freedom from financial worry.* She met Eros's gaze. *Oh, yes. Being with Eros is definitely a plus to this arrangement.*

Eros laughed heartily. "That *would* be another plus," he agreed pleasantly.

Pat bowed up as he put his mouth back to work on her, his tongue flicking against her vaginal walls in a sensuous dance. She grasped his hair, holding his head to her, torn between the urge to pull him over her and beg him to fill her and the orgasm teasing at her nerves.

The orgasm won out, slamming through her as if the last two had never happened. Pat groaned at the sensation. The need clawed at her, even in the midst of the mind-numbing pleasure Eros gave her.

"More convincing?" he asked, amusement coloring his voice.

"You read minds," she guessed, running her fingers through his hair.

"Hmmm? Yes. I do. Part of the job."

"Will I ache like this for you for the next millennium?" His hair was as soft as the silk beneath her.

His lips brushed over her clit again, and Pat closed her fist in his hair in response, fighting to normalize her ragged breathing.

"No. Only until you take your place," he assured her. "Well, the first week after you take your place, you will have a much higher sex drive than you usually will, but this maddening need will only last until you take your place."

"And...if I don't?"

His tongue traced the swollen seam. She screamed, her waning climax igniting again. Eros backed away. It took a moment for his words to make sense to her.

"You would never feel this way again. Even I am powerless to stop that. Even Jupe is. It is written in the stars, foretold by the Fates."

"I was born for you," she whispered.

Eros lifted her onto the bed and eased up beside her. "Yes. Yes you were." He kissed her, letting Pat taste herself in his mouth—the proof of his power over her pleasure.

Why would she ever give this up? *Never*, she decided.

Pat reached down, stroking his cock through his still-present Speedo, while he devoured her mouth. She pushed the suit away, in a fever for him.

He reads minds. He has to know I'm accepting him.

She circled her hand around his cock, moaning into his mouth.

Eros jerked, going still with his mouth parted from hers. "I cannot climax until I do so in you," he warned her.

"I don't want you to," she gasped out. Pat guided him toward her weeping core.

Eros turned her beneath him, running the head of his cock just inside her, using her lubrication and his, mixed, to tease her clit. "Be sure," he pleaded.

Pat writhed beneath him, moaning as he clasped her hip in one hand and held her still for more of his sensual torture.

"Now, Eros. Please. I'm sure."

"Soon. I have one final—"

"No! No more," she demanded.

He smiled. His cock wept more of his hot pre-cum, and he used it to massage her. "The forms state that I must give you your fondest wish. Ask anything of me, and I will deliver it before the night ends."

"Then you'll—" She bowed up, trying to capture his cock as Eros teased between her nether lips again.

He evaded her and went back to stroking at her clit. "Yes." His voice was hoarse.

Pat smiled at that. He was close to coming. She was sure of it. If she just—

"I cannot," he growled. "Choose, please. Before this drives us both mad." A hungry look stole over his features. "Or should I make you come again without me?"

She shook her head furiously. "I need," Pat gasped.

"Then choose!"

One look in his eyes convinced Pat that Eros was operating with a tenuous hold on his control.

Dozens of things flitted through her mind and were dismissed just as quickly. Why couldn't she think of anything to wish for? Why, when it was imperative that she come up with something, had her rational mind and even her creative center abandoned her?

Eros cursed fluently. "They always had years to decide. The consorts knew I would ask...until you."

Pat floundered, desperate for anything he wasn't already offering her. An image of Liz and Ben settled firmly in her mind. The moment was etched in her memories—the last time Pat had seen Ben alive.

"Don't be late, Pat," he called. "The wedding is at two."

Liz laughed from her place in the passenger seat. She batted at Ben's arm. "She won't be. We can't start without our Maid of Honor, you know."

Pat had waved them off. Later—much later, when she'd been sitting at Liz's hospital bedside, looking at her best friend's broken body—she'd mused that they'd tempted fate by going off together the night before the wedding.

She met Eros's gaze, gasping at the look of pain in the deep blue depths of his eyes.

"Choose again." It was a plea from a man—a god—who she didn't imagine begged for much of anything.

"You're a god. This can't be beyond you." It couldn't, could it?

"Trust me. Liz will have precisely what she needs. That has already—"

"She *needs* Ben," Pat insisted.

Eros seated the head of his cock inside her, holding her hips still with both hands. "She. Is. Taken. Care. Of. You need not waste your wish this way. I won't permit it. Now, trust me. Wish. Again."

Pat strained toward him without success. Her head spun, swimming with everything she'd thought she wanted yesterday or the day before, the month before... Most of them were part and parcel of being Eros's consort, and the rest seemed frivolous things to ask a god for, given the chance to ask for anything.

She went further, digging up wishes long forgotten, things she'd abandoned as unobtainable. Her mind locked on one, the one she'd thought she would never have.

Eros scanned his gaze down her body, as if he intended to lick her from head to toe like a Popsicle…and make her melt just as fast. "I have to deliver before the sun rises," he warned, as if that would dissuade her.

"You better." It came out slightly breathless, but she was sure he heard her. *Hell, he can read the thought from my mind.*

* * * *

Eros stroked his lips over hers, sending a fervent plea to Jupe and Hera. No consort had ever asked for this blessing before. It would take both their intercession to—

You have it. Their mental voices overlapped. Hera seemed amused by the request; Jupe was definitely irritated.

Eros didn't take the time to question that. "Done," he assured Patrice.

She closed her eyes, her breathing going ragged. Visions of them raising children together pushed her further toward release. Her rising climax beat at him.

"Not without me," he grumbled.

Patrice snapped her eyes open as he thrust into her. He stilled, giving her one last chance to refuse him.

"Now, Eros," she begged again.

He buried his hands in the wealth of her fiery curls, finding the pulse of her body seamlessly, matching his thrusts to the beat of her heart. She thrashed beneath him, her breathless cries echoing in the cavernous space around them.

Patrice wrapped her legs around his thighs, meeting his body's movements, her breathing hitching every time he lodged deep inside her. Her nails bit into his shoulders, dragging a groan of surprise and delight from him.

She met his gaze, her mental pleading silenced as her climax rolled through them both. He didn't hesitate to follow her over, drowning Patrice's scream with his roar of triumph.

As his seed pumped into her, Eros lost all his hold on the stored sum of her sexual energy, as he knew he would. The gold shimmering light surrounded them, skating over their sensitized skin and swirling in ever-widening circles.

Patrice watched the display breathlessly as the Love Blooms opened fully, their golden centers magnifying the release until it filled the dome above them. The golden globe of release shattered, scattering across the night sky like the stars beyond the dome. Several embers turned back, racing into the manor. The rising arousal from the rooms on the lower floors scorched along Eros's overtaxed nervous system.

He held his breath, his attention locked on one ember. It hovered for a few moments at the height of the dome. Then it dove straight down, piercing Patrice's body, sending a tremor through her womb…and Eros's body by extension.

She gasped, pressing a hand to the spot. "What was that?" she whispered, her voice filled with awe.

Eros covered her hand with his, but his wonder was in the knowing rather than the not knowing. "Your gift. The first of them, at any rate."

Her smile widened. "Really? Are you sure?"

"Considering the fact that a consort has never been pierced by her own release—"

"Her—? My release?"

He chuckled, turning his body until Patrice straddled his hips. "Without my consort, I am nothing. *My* power derives from our union." He laid a lick over her nipple playfully, smiling as aftershocks rocked her body. "You have limitless untapped potential, Patrice."

She looked up at the dome. "What does it do? When it—" She motioned vaguely at the cosmos.

"Helps people."

Patrice shot him a look of confusion, her brows drawing tight.

"Some of them will find lovers and toss them into a heated embrace or draw lovers closer. Some will find people who need a spot of kindness. And some—" He raised one of her hands and kissed her knuckles. "Some will find complete strangers destined for each other."

"You mean when we..." She blushed.

"Make love," he prompted her.

"Make love." The phrase was foreign to her, but it wouldn't be for long.

It's foreign to me, *now that I realize how I've devalued my consorts.*

"When we make love, we help people fall in love?" Patrice asked.

Eros nodded. "Or simply have a satisfying encounter, but I prefer to think about them finding love, especially when I have."

She beamed, her face lighting with an inner power. She sobered abruptly. "Wait. A consort has never... *None* of them wanted children? According to the myths—"

"Myths are written by humans. It only made sense to humans that a god of love and lust would have many children. In fact, I have never fathered a child. Until now.

"Why do you think Jupe and I have various names to choose from? It all depended on who was writing the myths. The names we use are immaterial; they are just convenient titles we adopt to interact with humans. I always preferred Eros—"

"Are you telling me I can't use the name Patrice Valentine?" she interrupted him.

She is going to challenge me at every turn. The thought warmed him. "If that is the name you want to use this century, by all means, use it."

"Mmmm." She smiled. "Oh, it is."

Patrice stroked a hand down his stomach suggestively, then licked her lips. "What happens if you climax but I don't."

Her seduction attempts are even better. "Why don't you find out," he invited.

She slid down his body, taking his cock into her mouth. Patrice groaned around him, responding to the phantom touches making her ready for him.

Her thought came to him clearly, making Eros laugh aloud. *Let's make someone happy.*

His laugh ended on a moan of pleasure. "Scores of them," he promised.

Chapter Six
The Ghost's Widow

"Go ahead, Liz. I'll...catch up soon."

Liz stared at Pat's retreating back, her heart heading north to a throbbing in her throat that would surely hit her head, given much more time. *Just what I need. A migraine, on top of everything else.*

Jupe offered his arm, playing the part of escort. "If you would, Ms. Reynolds?"

Pat turned the corner on the stairs, leaving Liz's field of vision. She didn't even look back. *She's leaving me. She promised she wouldn't leave me. What is she thinking? She broke her word to me, and Pat has never done that before.*

"Ms. Reynolds?" Jupe repeated.

She snapped her attention to him, noting his concern.

"Are you quite all right? We have a doctor on staff, if—"

"No." Liz forced a smile. "No. I'm fine. Really." She wasn't, but it would be easier to hide that if she took his arm and used Jupe for the slightest amount of balance.

He led her further into the structure, pointing out antique pieces, mostly from the Mediterranean area. The fifth time he called her Ms. Reynolds, Liz finally snapped.

"Call me Liz, please. Being called Ms. Reynolds makes me feel old." *And it's yet another reminder that I am not Mrs. Jessop.*

"As you wish." He motioned to the huge doorway before them. "This is the grand ballroom. You could have a cool drink here...or perhaps on the terrace beyond."

Liz took one look at the ballroom teeming with people. A glance out the open French doors showed the terrace was even more crowded. She swallowed hard and started to turn away. "I think I should go find Pat."

Jupe moved to intercept her. "Would you rather go to the buffet? I'm sure it would be less crowded, and you could get something to eat while you wait for Ms. Duberry to return."

"I don't know." Her stomach was in knots. How could she possibly eat? *Come up with* something *or he'll think you want to stay here.* "I promised to stay with Pat."

"More likely, she promised not to leave you." One sculpted brow went up in challenge.

Liz's cheeks heated in a flush. How did they know so much about her, and who was she going to have to kill for it?

His smile widened. "Come with me."

She stared at Jupe. Where was he going to take her?

"Liz?"

"I don't want a fantasy," she blurted out. Liz had enough of those already. Every time she closed her eyes, she had visions of being in Ben's arms again. Some days, she dreamed of joining him, and that idea was less than sane.

He sighed, seemingly worn. "I know. Look. Come with me, and we'll talk."

She hesitated, then nodded her agreement.

As he'd predicted, the buffet room was all-but deserted. Jupe led her to a comfortable-looking, padded armchair and helped her down into it. He settled on the one next to her. It was a long moment of potent silence before he started speaking.

"What would you say if I told you that bringing you here was mainly to ensure *Pat* accompanied you to the manor?"

The relief she felt at that pronouncement put her senses in a spin. Liz bit it back, mortified that she was glad it was Pat's head on the chopping block and not her own. "Really? So you're not trying to set me up with someone?" *Why am I asking? Can I trust anything he says?*

A rigid smile played at Jupe's lips. "There's no one for you but Ben."

Tears welled in her eyes. Though Liz had always said the same, it ripped her heart out to have someone besides Pat agree with her.

He doesn't even know me.

He knows so much it defies reason.

She argued that to avoid another startling thought. Had she secretly hoped Jupe would say there was someone else for her?

No. It couldn't be that.

"If you knew Pat had that one man for her, would you help her find him?"

"She's never mentioned a guy like that to me." If he was so right, Pat would have to know he was, and Liz thought Pat told her everything.

Oh, right. Like I tell her *everything?* She winced at that thought.

"Pat has never noticed her—"

That snapped Liz. "Just because a guy *says* he—"

"No no no no no no no." Jupe waved her off frantically. When Liz settled to hear him out, he sighed. Jupe took a moment to swivel his neck, a movement that ended in a resounding crack. "Now… Surely you've noticed that our research is exhaustive." He didn't question it.

That rankled, for some reason Liz couldn't put a name to. "It has occurred to me."

"Our matching is top notch."

"So…" She tried to work her way to his meaning. "You use some sort of software? An algorithm that matches interests and stuff like that?" If that was it, Liz wasn't sure she trusted it. She and Ben were definitely a case of opposites attracting.

"Nothing as simplistic as that. Interests may be enough to base a fling on, casual sex. Our clients hoping for love—for something more long-standing—require more substantial matching." He paused, then continued. "Often, the best of loves occur between people who share few interests. It's a very complex matter of psychology, background…even genetics."

"Genetics?" *He's kidding, right?*

Jupe nodded, his expression animated. "Studies have shown that lifelong relationships of people who have not been together since childhood or at least adolescence are largely based on a genetic compatibility." He waved her off before Liz could protest that it sounded like eugenics. "Some people describe it as the other person *smelling* right, which indicates individuals can smell genetic compatibility in the pheromones of others or some similar manner of recognizing the connection."

"And where, precisely, do you get these genetic—"

A roar of applause and cat-calling cut her off short. Liz glanced toward the windows overlooking the far side of the terrace. Her heart stuttered, and her mind rejected what she was seeing.

"Omigod." Liz pressed her hands to her face, horrified. What kind of place had she come to?

"Mr. Jupiter!"

He turned toward the server's voice, panned his gaze back to the windows, and jerked to his feet with a series of curses. "Please excuse me. I will return in a moment." Jupe loped for the door, then hesitated at the doorway to the ballroom and shot her a look of misery. "Believe me, this is not standard practice at the Fantasy Club."

Liz peeled her gaze from the couple who were fucking in clear view of everyone inside and on the terrace alike. She fidgeted, torn between the urge to leave the room and the urge to look that direction again.

Just to see if someone has broken it up or not, she assured herself.

Oh, this is insane. If the only reason she was here was to get Pat here, there was no reason for her to stay. Pat hadn't returned yet, which meant they might actually know what they were doing in match-making.

Even if they don't, Pat abandoned me, when she promised she wouldn't leave my side. It serves her right if I leave her here.

Resolved, Liz pushed to her feet and turned to leave.

For the second time in as many minutes, her mind had trouble processing what she was seeing. In a flash, it came into focus. Liz had just enough time to whisper Ben's name before everything went black.

Just before she lost consciousness, the sound of breaking glass rattled her nerves.

Chapter Seven

Ben saw her start to crumple and rushed toward Liz, cursing a blue streak. Asclepius reached her first. Of course, he was a demigod and had the ability to just pop into being wherever he needed to be.

"Let me," Ben grumbled, reaching for her.

"That may not be wise. At the very least, I should remove the shackles from her mind and body that weaken her before you approach her again."

"But, I—"

"Trust me. I will have Aceso and Hypnos assist me."

"Why did she see me?" he complained.

His brow lined in seeming confusion, he said, "I have no idea. It shouldn't have been possible. I suggest you speak to Hecate while I see to your lady."

"That may be a good idea. Let me know—"

"Of course." With that, he and Liz both disappeared.

Ben knew where he could find Hecate, of course. As the resident ghost or undead—whatever he could currently be classified as—she was his patron.

The basement of the manor was as lush as the rest of the building, but instead of gilded surfaces and white marble columns, the furniture was made of mahogany and dark cherry, the walls were made of basalt, and the metal hardware was made of pig iron. The rough walls and heavy wooden plank doors gave the feel of a dungeon, and there was a slight chill in the air. Few of the guests and clients required such trappings, and fewer of the gods would accept these surroundings, but Hecate seemed to thrive on it.

He knocked at her door, and a chorus of female voices invited him inside. Ben grimaced. It was always disconcerting to speak to Hecate; he was never sure which of her three forms to look at.

Ben let himself into her suite of rooms. He'd only taken a single step when deep growling brought him up short.

"Down, bitch!" one of the Hecates in the room ordered.

From the deep shadows of the back corner of the room, he saw a massive black shaggy dog drop to her stomach and rest her head on her paws. A skunk toddled across the back of the room and settled beside her.

Friend? Companion? Fellow sufferer?

"Well, come in, Benjamin," a sweet-voiced one invited.

Morning? He could rarely tell her apart from Mid-day, unless the trio was distressed.

"Shut that door. The light offends me," another continued.

Definitely Evening. That one is always a bit cranky. He did as she commanded. It never served a person well to piss off Hecate. *Any of her three forms.*

It didn't surprise him that the light from the hallway, weak as it was when compared to the light upstairs, hurt her eyes. Her lush rooms were only lit by a single torch each on two opposing walls of every room. The torches lit as she entered rooms and extinguished as she left them, even if that left a supplicant in utter darkness. He suspected at least one of her forms enjoyed doing that to humans.

The darkness made identifying her three forms even harder. Not only did the women—*or would it be woman?*—look identical, their clothing were the same cut of floor-length dress in three very dark colors that were impossible to tell apart in the dim light: garnet red for Morning, pine green for Mid-day, and midnight blue for Evening. Or so he'd been told.

She didn't wait for him to find the words to address her. All three voices addressed him at once. "You want to know why Elizabeth could see you."

"How could she?" He tried to rein in his frustration. "I was told she wouldn't, until the time was right. If this fails—"

"I made a deal with you, boy."

That could have been any of them. If he pissed her off, Hecate was all pissed off, not just one-third. He didn't press his luck by responding.

A calmer voice continued, and his heart eased. She wasn't one hundred percent pissed off, if any of them responded calmly. As far as he could tell, all three had to agree to obliterate someone for you to end up like Hecate's two *pets*.

Let's not test that theory.

"I take my deals very seriously. You may not be able to bank on my moods, but one thing you *can* bank on is that I will do everything in my power to keep to a deal."

"Or release the entire deal," Evening finished.

It was a veiled warning at best. If Hecate released him, he and Liz would both suffer until the day she died. He reminded himself to play the supplicant as well as he could.

"Please explain this. I need to understand what went wrong. Was it something I did?"

There was a moment of silence. When she replied, it was Morning addressing him.

"On occasion, the gods' magic interferes with each other's. Another god did something that clashed with our magic."

"It was Eros. You know it was," Evening snapped.

"Why would Eros interfere? He's part of the deal," Ben said. None of this made sense.

All three women turned to look at him. None of them spoke for a moment.

"It doesn't matter." Evening brushed off the question.

Mid-day took up the reply from there. "Jupiter has let him know to avoid the issue again. We should have no more problems."

No more problems. That's good to hear. Ben shook himself mentally. That didn't mean this would go off without a hitch.

"Go now. The healing is complete. Hypnos says she should sleep for a few more minutes. The rest is largely up to you, Benjamin."

His heart tripped in equal amounts of excitement and fear. He dipped his head in a bow and headed for the door. "Thank you for seeing me, Hecate."

"We were glad to set your mind at ease," Morning offered brightly.

"Proceed with caution," Mid-Day added in warning.

"Don't come back unless it's important," Evening snapped.

Ben stopped in surprise, glancing back at them. Two of the forms stared at the third. One was gaping in open-mouthed horror. *Morning.* The other was glaring a warning. *Mid-day.*

The third spoke. "Please." It was said in a curt, irritated tone, but it still softened her warning somewhat.

"I will try my best not to offend, Hecate." With that, Ben slipped out the door and closed it behind him.

He hurried along, unsure of how much time had passed. He'd learned long ago that time spent in a god's quarters might not match the passage of time outside of them. Some gods regulated that to match human sensibilities when dealing with a human guest. Hecate didn't. He might have been in there ten minutes or five hours. He had no way of knowing for sure.

Then again, that might be a blessing. If it was *hours, it would have been maddening to wait all that time for news of Liz. This way, it seems like minutes, even if it wasn't.*

He was halfway up the stairs to the main floor before his lips curved in a smile at another thought. *I did it. I figured out who all three were this time.*

Of course, I have to start all over again next time I see Hecate. He secretly wondered if she did that just to keep people unbalanced in her presence. *Maybe not consciously,* he conceded. *It's part of her mystique.*

The distance to the room Jupe had assigned to Liz passed in a blur. Ben wasn't sure if he was running or just lost in thought, but in what seemed like moments, he was standing outside the door.

Listening to the sweet sounds of her voice.

* * * *

Liz stretched, sighing as no wrenching pains brought her up short. *As usual.* Her brow furrowed. Somehow, she'd ended up in bed. She was still wearing her dress, though her shoes were off. Other sensations made her take inventory. Was she surrounded by silk?

"Oh, good. You're awake," a strange voice addressed her.

She snapped upright, wincing in the expectation of complaints from her injuries. *Again...nothing.*

Hands closed around her shoulders. "Slowly. We don't want you collapsing again."

Her eyes focused with excruciating slowness. Whoever he was, he was tall and dark-haired, slim and athletic. Unlike the guests and staff downstairs, he was dressed in a crisp collared shirt, his tie loosened to allow him a small vee of open buttons.

Liz extricated herself from his hold, trying not to offend him but also uncomfortable with him touching her. "Who are you?" She didn't question *where* she was. Clearly, this was a room in the Fantasy Club.

"I'm the head physician here at the manor. Everyone calls me Doctor A. Or Ace. Whichever you prefer. I'm not picky." He reached down and placed his hand on her wrist.

Taking my pulse? But he's not timing it?

Ace straightened, then smiled. "That's much better. How does your head feel?"

"Fine." *Why would he ask that?* "Did I hit it or something?"

"Oh, no. Nothing like that. It's just that I was told you suffer from migraines, and—"

"By whom?" Someone was going to get slammed with a HIPAA suit.

He smiled and tapped the MedicAlert bracelet she wore.

"Oh…yes. I forgot." Her cheeks flamed. "Sorry about that."

"Not at all."

Liz looked around, admiring the décor of the room. It reminded her of reproductions of Victorian-age American homes.

"Now… Do you remember what happened?"

She nodded, remaining silent. It was the last thing Liz wanted to think about.

Ace sighed. "You're not going crazy, Elizabeth."

"Excuse me?" His look was earnest, and as much as she wanted to shout him down, she wasn't sure he was pulling a scam on her.

He settled in a chair pulled to the bedside, then steepled his fingers in front of his face. "You saw Ben down there. Didn't you?"

Words stuck in her throat. When they finally emerged, the need to run came with them. "I should go."

He raised his hands and motioned her back, his expression brooking no argument. "With Pat here, there is no one to keep an eye on you at home."

"I'm sure I don't need—"

"It is my professional opinion that you do," he informed her.

"Seriously? You're really going to keep me here?"

Ace sighed. "Just for the night. In the morning, you can have breakfast with Pat and be on your way, if that is what you wish. In the meantime, I've taken the liberty of ordering dinner for you."

Liz opened her mouth to offer an excuse that she had to be home… *For some reason.*

"Besides that, I haven't finished explaining why you saw Ben."

And then there's that. She wondered what the best way to tell someone he was insane without angering him was.

Ace laughed. "I assure you, I am not insane. Neither are you."

Her throat went dry, and her heart thudded in her chest. A weak laugh escaped her lips. "I wouldn't bet on that last part. Look… I know Jupe said there was no one for me but Ben, but I really don't want a hologram or whatever hocus pocus you're offering. It won't be Ben."

"But it is. It is the Ben you remember. I promise you that."

He seemed so sincere, Liz allowed herself to hope. Anger that she'd gone there was hot on its heels, and memories of where her discussion with Jupe had been interrupted made her heart stutter. *Genetics.* "Even if there was some way to clone Ben, it wouldn't *be* Ben. It would just be genetically similar to him."

Ace scowled. "He's not a clone. I have no clue why I thought I would just be able to explain this to you. Let me bring in Ben, and he can explain it for himself."

Forcing her jaw to unlock was more difficult than it should have been. "Fine. Show *it* in." *I'll prove it's not Ben, and this insanity will be over.*

At which point, I will spend the rest of my life nursing the hurt, because I believed it was possible for just a moment.

"Him." He waved her off before she could retort. "I'll let him handle this."

With that, Ace stood and ambled to the door. He opened it and spoke quietly to someone on the other side.

That thing. *Whatever it is.* She crossed her arms over her chest.

"Fine. I'll leave you to it, then," Ace announced, his jovial nature back in full swing.

"Thank you for your help."

Oh, God. It sounds like Ben, too. How am I going to survive this?

Chapter Eight

The sight of her ripped at his heart. It wasn't just missing Liz, though that had been hell on Little Olympus. It was the slight quiver of her lips, the sheen of tears in her eyes, the way she held herself—arms wrapped tightly around her chest, as if she felt she would fly apart.

He felt the same way, but there was no time for that. Her misery shredded him, and he had to stop that as soon as possible.

Ben made his way toward the chair, then revised that and settled lightly on the edge of the bed. Liz started to edge away then stopped, her jaw tightening.

She didn't give him a chance to speak. "You're *not* Ben. You can't be."

What had seemed simple in planning now loomed over him as an insurmountable obstacle. How could he explain this? "I am. I can prove to you that I'm Ben." *I have to. Otherwise, this whole thing goes down the toilet.*

"How? By telling me when I was born or what my favorite color is?" she snapped at him. Her lip curled in an expression he never thought he would see from Liz.

Let alone aimed at me. Disdain.

"Anyone could come up with those things," he agreed. "Even telling you what your computer password is or mentioning Ruff the mutt dog you had when you were a child wouldn't do the trick. Too many cases of identity theft prove it's not impossible to learn those things."

"Then what?" she challenged. "How do you intend to convince me?"

It wasn't hard to decide. "Maybe by telling you what you said to me after the first time we made love?"

Her breathing hitched, and her eyes dilated in shock, but she didn't say anything to dissuade him.

"In your bed, wrapped in the quilt your grandmother made, the one you only bring out when you're sick or when you want to spruce up the room. You put your hand on my chest and you had the most devilish smile on your lips. You told me you were sure it was a fluke and demanded to—"

"What are you? An identical cousin or something? Ben told you that. He had to have told you that." Her voice pitched up in near panic.

Ben sighed. "You know all my family, Liz. You know I don't have any male cousins, and my brothers don't look like me. It's me. It really is."

She motioned shakily with one hand, up and down his body. "You're *not* Ben. You can't be. I saw you die."

He winced. "Yes. And I remember the last thing you said to me."

Her face lost all color. "Don't. Please don't."

Ben powered through. He had to prove this to her. "Come back to me, Ben. Whatever it takes, come back to me."

Silence fell between them. A single tear trailed down her cheek.

"I couldn't promise you that I would then, but in a strange turn of fate, it was possible…to an extent."

"What—?" Liz snapped her mouth shut.

Probably reminding herself not to believe. "What extent?" He sighed and pushed a hand back through his hair. *I will never get used to the idea of having a physical form again.*

Her jaw dropped, and her hand twitched, as if she wanted to touch him.

She recognizes the way I move.

Back to the subject. "I only have a physical body here in Little Olympus. I cannot leave here, but you can be with me here." He waved her off before she could speak. "We can move all of your belongings to my house on the grounds, if you still want to be with me." They had planned to move to an apartment together anyway. *A house, once we had children.*

"Wait. What…? I mean, how…?" Confusion clouded her expression.

"It's hard to explain, but…" Ben took a deep breath, reveling in the scent of her perfume. "This place is called Little Olympus for a reason. Jupe… Jack Jupiter really is Zeus or Jupiter or whatever name he's going by today. Eric Valentine really is Eros or Cupid. Ace?" He motioned to the door. "Asclepius, the son of Apollo. Haven't met *him* yet. He tends to hang out on Olympus, I guess."

Her brow furrowed, and her cheek pulled in a look of speculation and disbelief. "You're saying you've met gods and they live here?"

Ben nodded. "Hecate, Ares, Diana, Minerva, Dis Pater…oh, and Loki." He grimaced. "Yeah, he's a real joker in a dark sort of way. If someone believes it—really believes it—the god or goddess probably exists.

"You have met some of them too. They don't all live here. Some just have rooms here and visit. Eros lives here full time. Most of the others I've met don't."

"Okay. This is insane."

"More insane than me being here. Here…take my hand." He extended it toward her. Though he didn't want to shock her with touching her unexpectedly, he was running out of ways to prove he was real.

Liz hesitated. She reached out, a tentative move at best, and stroked her fingers along the bowl of his palm. Shivers of pleasure raced down his spine in response.

"Gods. Magic," he whispered. "It's all true. I'm not lying to you."

She didn't withdraw. Liz traced her fingertips along the lines of his fingers, seemingly comparing them to what she remembered.

You won't find differences.

"But why? I don't understand what makes us important enough to do this for. People die, and they are gone." She shot him a quelling look. "You didn't sell your soul or something, did you?"

He couldn't help himself. Ben laughed, long and hard, catching her fingers with his as he'd done so often. When he recovered enough, he shook his head. "No. Nothing like that. Simply put, we were lucky enough to have friends in high places."

"I don't understand. Neither of us have friends in high places, as far as I know."

"Jupe told you about Pat's intended love?"

She nodded, but it was a tense move.

"It's… Well, it's sort of a house rule that no one gets invited to Little Olympus unless he or she is either a client or a guest."

Liz worked at words that didn't immediately emerge. When they did, they came out in a rush. "They needed me to get Pat here, so I *had* to have a fantasy as well? And since Jupe said there's no one for me but you—"

"That's how it worked," he agreed, relieved that she seemed to be accepting what he was telling her.

"You're really Ben, and I can be with you, if we live on the grounds." Something in her tone said she wasn't accepting this at all.

"Yes."

"I'm still unconscious. I hit my head. I'm hallucinating, and—"

"No. None of that is true. What I'm telling you is the truth." *Why was none of this working out as it was supposed to?*

Inspiration struck. Ace said he was going to heal Liz. "Are you in any pain?"

"More proof that this is a dream," she huffed.

"Maybe. Maybe not. Ace healed your wounds. It's part of his magic. The fantasy involves us being together as much like we were before as possible. No scars. No migraines. No—"

"Now I know I'm dreaming." Still, Liz moved her hand to a place under her hair, her eyes widening.

"Do you want me to pinch you to prove you're not dreaming?" he teased.

"Say for argument that this is real..."

Ben waited patiently for her to continue. She had to come to terms with this in her own way.

"What happens now?"

"That depends on you." This was the most difficult part, as far as he was concerned. *And I thought the last part was difficult? I'm an idiot.*

"If you're real, I'm not leaving," Liz informed him hotly.

He smiled. "I was hoping that would be the case. As it stands, I'm immortal on these grounds, and you are mortal. That means we have a couple of choices."

She swallowed hard, then nodded. "And those are?"

"We could live out your lifetime here, you remaining mortal. You could leave the grounds whenever you like and come back, but I would be here. You would age and die as you are meant to, barring some accident. When you die, I could choose to join you in the afterlife."

"But I continue to age, and I assume you don't." She didn't question it.

Fast learner. "That is a difficulty, I admit. I know I would still love you, but you might be self-conscious about looking decades older than I do."

"I assume the other choice is that I die and join you?"

He winced at the fear in her voice. "Probably not the way you think. We actually have two more choices.

"The first *would* be you choosing to take Hecate's potion tonight. You would be in the same state I am, immortal, here with me."

"While all of our friends and family die off," she added sadly.

Ben didn't answer that. He knew well enough that at least one friend would hopefully be around for as long as they were, but it wasn't his place to tell Liz that.

"The second option is a hybrid of the two. You could remain mortal for a period of time and then choose to drink Hecate's potion later."

She stared at him, seemingly at a loss for words. Ben let her find them at her own pace.

"And what difference would that make?" she demanded.

A sly smile curved his lips up. Ben couldn't have held it back if he wanted to. "I have a physical body here. We could have the children we'd planned to."

Her mouth gaped open.

"If you still want to," he conceded. Ben was fairly certain he knew the answer to that, but it was still better to say it and let her decide.

She was slow responding, and his nerves jumped and shimmied in warning.

"How do we explain all this to our friends and family?"

He chuckled. "You forget that we have gods on our side. Mnemosyne can rewrite memories. Jupe can have a whole team erase physical proof of my death from their homes. We can come up with some sort of excuse for people to visit us here."

For an agonizing moment, she was still and silent. Just when Ben was starting to worry, Liz launched herself into his arms and kissed him.

A heartbeat later, the rush of lust hit him full force. Ben closed his eyes and savored it.

My gods, it worked! Pat has taken her place with Eros.

* * * *

Children? With Ben? The life we'd planned, more or less? Liz could kiss him for coming back to her.

As if that thought summoned some godly force, the sudden need to do more than kiss him swamped her. Without thought, Liz wrapped her arms around him and kissed Ben.

He groaned, opening to her, their tongues dueling. The heat rose between them, ratcheting up as he slid the zipper at the back of her dress down. She went to work on the buttons on his shirt. In moments, the dress was down to her elbows, and one of Ben's hands cupped a breast, massaging the nipple up.

Their mouths parted, and they gasped in each other's expelled air.

"Gods damn this," Ben breathed. He lowered his head and sucked in the opposite nipple, wrenching a cry of delight from her.

Liz shook the dress off her arms and grasped the back of his head. Ben dragged the open shirt off, then pulled the dress down to her thighs. He took a moment to stroke at her clit though her panties, leaving her gasping in response.

"Like the panties you wore with this last time," he informed her.

She nodded in agreement. Those had been crotchless panties. *How could I possibly know they would be a good idea tonight?* Liz hadn't expected to be having sex, after all.

"Have to get them off," he continued in the broken speech patterns he fell into when he was really excited.

Liz worked her teeth against her lower lip as he stripped off her dress and panties together. Ben didn't bother with her thigh-high stockings, save to run his hands up the insides of them with a murmur of approval.

In the next second, he was popping his pants open and shoving them down his thighs. A heartbeat later, he was inside her, both of them shouting.

Her hands closed into fists in his hair, and his settled at her buttocks as he thrust into her again. Liz moved her legs to a comfortable position over his thighs, positioning herself more centered around him.

Memories of the cruise they took to Bermuda danced in her mind. One steamy night, they'd made love—just like this—the balcony door open to the island sounds and scents.

"Gods, yes." Ben thrust harder and faster, seemingly reliving the same memory she was.

The rest passed in a haze of sensation. At her climax, he joined her, his entire body stiffening, then jerking. It was a sure sign Ben enjoyed it as much as she did.

That was the only coherent thought she had. Everything else was a patchwork of sensation. Their sweat-soaked chests tantalized Liz, bringing her nipples to almost painful points against his chest hair. She was wrapped around him. Their lips brushed, joined, parted, and repeated.

Just when she thought it was over, a new wave of lust washed over her, and Liz started moving her hips against him, riding his renewed erection. Ben joined in the dance.

That time, they took longer to come, but no sooner had they slowed than they were moving again, changing positions, hands exploring. At the third climax, Liz panted out the same refrain Ben had been all along.

"Oh, gods."

The need to have more of him came nearly on the heels of that plea.

"Damn right," Ben agreed.

Chapter Nine

Liz accompanied Ben into "private dining room" on the top floor of the manor, just below the dome. He'd said there was a possibility Eros and his consort might invite them up to the dome to see it later. While that sounded interesting, what she really wanted was time with Ben.

After their marathon of sex the night before, Liz was slightly amazed she could walk straight, and Ben's sappy smile said he was as energized as she was by it. Still, they had to eat. The only reason they'd left the room was Ben's insistence on joining the breakfast party.

Unlike the buffet downstairs, this room was set for no more than a dozen and a half people. There were only four at the table when they entered the room, two couples at the head and foot of the table. Jupe was the only one she recognized.

"Well, good morning," the red-head at his side welcomed them.

"Good morning," Liz offered brightly in reply, though she didn't know who the woman was.

The other couple didn't add verbal greetings. The man tipped his head in greeting, and the woman with him waved. Liz returned the wave with a smile. She wasn't sure what the protocol was for the Fantasy Club, but she suspected it included *not* asking other guests what their fantasy had been.

"Ares," Ben addressed the man.

He grunted out a reply. The woman with him shot him a glare, and he sighed.

"Good morning, Ben. Liz."

His partner leaned toward him and kissed his cheek, prompting a smile from the gruff individual.

"Did you have a good evening?" Jupe questioned. By his raised eyebrow, Liz could tell he was supremely pleased she had.

Well, he is a god. Might as well stroke his ego. "Another for the memory books."

Ben wrapped an arm around her waist and placed a kiss on her cheek. His erection pressed against her buttocks, through his jeans and the light dress that had appeared in their room that morning.

Knee-length dresses, and I have no scars to make me self-conscious about wearing one anymore.

"Thank you," Ben addressed their host.

Jupe scowled. "I may be head of the household, but you know as well as I do that Eros is your true host at the Fantasy Club."

As if his name summoned him, Eric Valentine—*Eros*—entered the room through the far door.

With Pat on his arm.

Liz's mind locked on all the things Ben had told her. "*You're* Eros's consort?"

"We prefer wife," Eros replied with a tip of his head. "Welcome to the manor, Liz."

It took a moment for Pat's expression to make it through Liz's shock. Her eyes went from wide to brimming with tears. She pressed a trembling hand to her lips. At last, she lowered it.

"Y-you did this for them?" Pat asked.

Eros chuckled darkly. "You did, my dear. I only spoke to a few key gods. It was your magic—"

He didn't make it any further. Pat turned toward him and pulled Eros into a full-out carnal kiss that left no doubts to the fact that she'd latched on to the one right man for her.

The passion curling in Liz's stomach made her gasp in surprise. She glanced around, watching as the woman beside Jupe started undoing buttons on his shirt. At the opposite end of the table, Ares and his woman were already engaged in pulling at each other's clothing.

Jupe growled out something she didn't understand. "The next week is going to be interesting." With that, he motioned sharply.

Liz found herself back in their room, naked. Before she could decide if she should cover herself or not, she and Ben were locked in a heated embrace. He folded her over the high mattress and started thrusting from behind.

It was over in moments, leaving them gasping and then giggling.

Liz recovered first. "So when Pat gets…excited…?"

"Yep. But only for the first week of being his consort. Or so I've been told."

"So that was just her—"

"Hell, no. I would be all over you anyway, given the opportunity." As if in confirmation, his cock bucked against her sheath.

They parted slowly, and Ben lifted her to the bed, his eyes glittering in mischief.

Liz sighed. "We are going to starve in the next week. Aren't we?" She didn't really care if they did. Eternity with Ben would decidedly be worth it, either way.

As if by magic—*and it probably was*—a large tray appeared on top of the bureau along the far wall of the room.

She laughed, and Ben joined in.

"Welcome to the Fantasy Club," he announced, "where all of your fantasies and wishes come true." Ben pressed his lips to hers. "Most of mine have."

"Mine too."

"Not quite yet," he answered cryptically.

It took a moment for her to catch up with him. "Oh, you mean a baby."

"That too. I actually meant our wedding…if you're still interested in marrying me."

She brushed her lips to his, warming from the inside. "Maybe we should have a double wedding. The two of us, Pat and Eros."

He seemed to consider that for a moment. "He did say they prefer the term wife to consort. We can talk to them about it later."

Pleasure curled inside her. "Much later. We *are* going to starve."

"Breakfast will keep. I want you." His lips closed over hers. *Forever.*

Fill in the blanks between what happened in *The Consort* with the upcoming books in the series! Where did Jupe go when he left Liz?

About the Author

Brenna Lyons wears many hats, sometimes all on the same day: former president of EPIC, author of more than 100 published works, owner of Fireborn Publishing, columnist, special needs teacher, wife, mother...and member in good standing of more than 60 writing advocacy groups.

In her first ten years published in novel-length, she won 3 EPIC e-Book Awards (out of 15 finalists) and finaled for 3 PEARLS (including one Honorable Mention, second to NY Times Bestseller Angela Knight), 2 CAPAS, and a Dream Realm Award. She's also taken Spinetingler's Book of the Year for 2007.

Brenna writes in 27 established worlds plus stand-alones, poetry, articles and essays. She's a bestseller in indie/e fantasy and horror, straight genre and cross-genres thereof. Brenna has been termed "one of the most deviant erotic minds in the publishing world...not for the weak." (Rachelle for Fallen Angels Reviews) Milieu-heavy dark work is practically Brenna's calling card, with or without the erotic content. She teaches classes in everything from POV studies to advanced editing, networking to marketing. Brenna enjoys hearing from people who read her work and can be reached by e-mail.

Website: http://www.brennalyons.com/

Facebook: http://www.facebook.com/brenna.lyons

Email: brennalyons4168@live.com

Magmon's Lover

KEGIN
Conquest
The Last of Fion's Daughters
Last Chance for Love
Rites of Mating
In Her Ladyship's Service
Matchmaker's Misery

KIELAN
The Lady's Lowborn Lover
Time Currents
Cubed

NIGHT WARRIORS
Night Warriors
Will of the Stone
Bearing Armen
Hunter's Moon
Maher Men
The Warrior's Man
Damsel in Distress
Choosing a Mate/Starting a War
Raised to be His Own
Veriel's Tales: Crossbearer Turned
Veriel's Tales II: Losing Regana
Blutjagdfrau Lost

XXAN WAR
Daahn Rising
Crossbred Son
Raashh Decisions

All I Want for Christmas is You
All's Fair...

And it was Good
Animal Instincts
Black Sail
Dream Walk
Enslaved
Fates War
Mama's Tales
Marked
May the Best Man Win
Nevermore
The Color of Love (paired with a free read titled A Safe Heart)
Unexpected Daddy
We Shall Live Again

With **Mundania Press**

STAR MAGES
Written in the Stars
The Master's Lover

Fairy Dreams
Monsters of Myth

With **Under the Moon**

RENEGADES
Tygers
Renegade's Run
Max Sec

URBAN GRIMM
Catch Me, If You Can
Three Wishes
Temptation of Eve

With Great Power
Undead Underway

ANTHOLGIES WITH UTM
Evil Overlords' Union Issue #1
Forbidden Love: Bad Boys
Forbidden Love: Sacred Bands
Forbidden Love: Wicked Women
Undead Embrace

With **Logical Lust**

"Mine for the Night" in The Cougar Book

With **Coming Together** Charity Anthologies

"Claim Mate" in Coming Together: Against the Odds
"Foundling" in Coming Together: Into the Light
"The Fire God's Woman" in Coming Together: Under Fire

Self-published (most available from **Fireborn Publishing**)

KEGIN
Earth-Born Lord
Graham: Traning the Earth-Born Lord

NIGHT WARRIORS
Stone Lord
Claiming a Lady

PROPHECY
Prophecy: Revelations
Prophecy: Rapture